BOOK
2

MEET ME AT MIDNIGHT

BOOK
2

MEET ME AT MIDNIGHT

JENNIFER TORRES

Scholastic Inc.

For my nina, Tricia

Copyright © 2023 by Jennifer Torres

All rights reserved. Published by Scholastic Inc., *Publishers since 1920.* SCHOLASTIC and associated logos are trademarks and/or registered trademarks of Scholastic Inc.

The publisher does not have any control over and does not assume any responsibility for author or third-party websites or their content.

No part of this publication may be reproduced, stored in a retrieval system, or transmitted in any form or by any means, electronic, mechanical, photocopying, recording, or otherwise, without written permission of the publisher. For information regarding permission, write to Scholastic Inc., Attention: Permissions Department, 557 Broadway, New York, NY 10012.

This book is a work of fiction. Names, characters, places, and incidents are either the product of the author's imagination or are used fictitiously, and any resemblance to actual persons, living or dead, business establishments, events, or locales is entirely coincidental.

ISBN 978-1-338-83317-1

10 9 8 7 6 5 4 3 2 1   23 24 25 26 27

Printed in the U.S.A.   40
First printing 2023

Book design by Maeve Norton

CHAPTER 1

Sunlight spills through the stained glass windows of the study and scatters splotches of color—seafoam and moss and evergreen—on the walls and carpets.

Dalia squints. Someone ought to hang some curtains in here. She wriggles deeper into her chair, rich green velvet with a high, tufted back. She curls her legs onto the cushion.

"Wouldn't it be more comfortable if you took your boots off?" Princesa Carmen asks, looking up from the round oak table where the other first-year princesas in Casita Emerald are studying maps. "Not to mention cleaner," she mutters.

Dalia does not answer. She finds that when people talk, they usually aren't talking to her. Most of the time, she fades into the background. Most of the time, you can forget she's even there.

Or at least that was how it used to be. Before she walked through the golden gates of the Fine and Ancient Institute for the Royal, an academy for princesas in training. Here, it is becoming almost impossible to disappear.

"Dalia?" Princesa Eloísa says, lifting her head too. "Your boots?"

Dalia looks down at the scuffed toe of one of her boots. It peeks out from under the hem of her gown, the same deep and dangerous gray of a thundercloud. "No, I think I'll leave them on." She pauses. She pushes her dark curls out of her eyes and straightens the tiara she received on her first day. It has silver points like owl talons, a teardrop-shaped emerald atop each one. "A princesa should always be prepared, don't you agree?"

Carmen and Eloísa shrug and bend their heads over the maps again.

"What we *should* be preparing for is the Geography exam," Carmen says.

"We can get through the Realms of Moonlit Snow before the dinner bells," Princesa Marisol, sitting at the head of the table, suggests.

"And save the Lands of Whispering Wind for tomorrow," Eloísa agrees.

When she is sure the princesas are focused on their studies again, Dalia taps her fingernail softly against her boot. "Don't worry, Don Ignacio," the gentle rhythm tells the lizard hiding inside. "I'll never let them find you." Don Ignacio flicks his tongue on her ankle in ticklish reply, and Dalia has to swallow a giggle.

The lizard isn't the only thing Dalia is hiding. She picks up the heavy geography book on her lap and opens it. Concealed in its pages, where the princesas can't see them, are her letters from the Bewitched Academy for the Dreadful. The infamous school for villains. The place where Dalia truly belongs.

That is, she's sure she *would* belong there, if only she could get in.

Blurry through the stained glass window, she can just make out the B.A.D.'s mysterious towers rising over the clouds, no more than a day's walk away. Yet reading over these letters, the academy seems farther from her than ever.

Your plot was perfectly unpleasant, but only fairly dreadful.

The scheme was somewhat surprising, yet not nearly dreadful enough.

Creative, but still not particularly dreadful.

Rejection after rejection. The B.A.D. is notoriously selective. Only the most terrifyingly talented young villains are admitted. By now, Dalia has read the letters so many times she knows them by heart. Yet she studies them still, hoping to find some clue inside, something she hasn't noticed before, that will show her how she can prove she is dreadful enough to be welcomed there. Welcomed home.

She touches the locket, encrusted with black opals, that her abuelos gave her before sending her off to the F.A.I.R., insisting it was the best place for her. That she would grow to love it. The warm stones shimmer with threads of gold and violet and blue.

"I've never seen black opals before," Eloísa says. "Where did the necklace come from?"

Dalia startles. These princesas have turned out to be far more observant than she imagined they'd be.

"Nowhere," Dalia says, dropping the locket under the beaded neckline of her gown, where she usually keeps it.

"*Nowhere?*" Eloísa wrinkles her freckled nose

and tilts her head so that her own tiara—five slender gold bands, dotted with round emeralds like musical notes—slips.

"I mean, from home," Dalia replies.

"It's too bad you didn't get an *emerald* locket instead," Carmen says, scribbling on a scroll. "Or that you weren't placed in Casita Opal."

On the day they arrived, Profesora Colibrí, the F.A.I.R.'s head teacher, assigned each of the first-year princesas to a Casita: Emerald, Sapphire, Ruby, or Opal.

"*Carmen!*" Eloísa objects. "Dalia belongs in Casita Emerald. With us."

Dalia pulls the book closer. She lets her curls fall over her eyes and hopes the princesas will go back to ignoring her again.

Instead, to her horror, Eloísa stands. She smooths the wrinkles on her green satin pants, gold embroidery shimmering on each leg. She steps toward Dalia's chair.

"What are you working on anyway?" Eloísa asks. She wears a matching vest and jacket and a floppy bow tie made of ivory silk. She peers over Dalia's book. "Don't you want to come over and study with us? Everything's more fun with other people. Even geography."

Dalia slams the book shut. Don Ignacio squirms inside her boot. "Sorry about that," she whispers.

"Huh?" Eloísa tilts her head again.

"Nothing," Dalia says. She blows the hair out of her eyes and swings her feet to the ground, carefully, so as not to disturb Don Ignacio. "And anyway, I was just leaving." She tucks the geography book, letters stashed inside, under her arm. She doubts that anything is really more fun with other people. Most of the time, the fun wears off quickly. As soon as those other people think they know her.

There has only been one exception. Dominga.

Dominga was assigned to Casita Opal, but really, she's a villain too and just as desperate as Dalia is to break free from the palace. Together, they hope to hatch a scheme horrible enough to gain admission to the B.A.D. In fact, they are planning one this very evening.

"Leaving?" Eloísa asks. "Did you forget something in the suite? I'll go with you. I need to change for dinner anyway." She touches the silk bow. "I always end up spilling chocolate sauce on my moño."

Dalia did not expect the princesas to be so very . . . persistent. This is not going to be as easy as she thought. But then, nothing has been.

"I'm on my way to the bakery," Dalia replies.

"Chef Luís-Esteban said I could have the stale palmeras to feed the crows."

Eloísa shudders. "Chef Luís-Esteban scares me. He's always so grumpy."

It is exactly what Dalia hoped she'd say. And exactly why she likes Chef Luís-Esteban.

"Ask him to make more of those jalapeño empanadas," Carmen calls out from the table.

Dalia grinds her teeth. She and Dominga were the ones who stirred the jalapeños into the apple empanada filling. They were supposed to have been a secret—and *wicked*—addition to the chef's recipe. But in the end, the princesas loved them. Instead of begging for water to soothe their burning tongues, they lined up for second helpings.

Dalia and Dominga cannot fail again.

"Don't worry," Dalia says. "I'll make sure there's something *extra* special on the menu for dinner."

She slips out the door and manages to hold in her cackle until it closes behind her.

CHAPTER 2

After dropping her book off in the bedroom suite, Dalia considers how to get to the palace bakery. The fastest way is outside, through a sunken garden filled with towering shrubs. Each is trimmed to illustrate a scene from a fairy tale. A girl soaring on the back of an eagle to rescue a wounded prince. A daughter of the Dragon Palace standing on the shore and summoning horses from the sea. A princesa knitting nettles into vests to save her eleven brothers, who have been turned by a witch into swans.

The shrubs, Profesora Colibrí has said, are reminders of courage, cleverness, and kindness. The traits of a true princesa. "Study them well," she told them. "Discover the lessons they hold."

(*There are lessons to learn from villains too*, Dalia had thought. *Daring. Dedication. Danger.* But she hardly expects the princesas will appreciate any of those.)

The gate to the garden will be locked now that it's after sunset. Even if Dalia picked the lock—which she knows how to do, of course—she would be caught. Or worse, asked by Señor De La Rosa, the gardening instructor, to help gather a bouquet of the flowers that bloom year-round in the colors of each Casita: red sweet peas, green bells of Ireland, blue butterfly bush, and white gardenias. Just imagining their too-sweet smells makes Dalia's stomach turn.

Luckily, Dominga's sister, Princesa Paloma, gave Dominga a diary with a hand-drawn map of the palace inside. (Dominga calls it her spell book.) Paloma was a student at the F.A.I.R. And not just any student. When she graduated last year, Paloma was named the Fairest of the F.A.I.R., the most perfect of all the princesas. *So* perfect that Dalia can't quite work out how she managed to find the secret tunnel that leads from the suites to the bakery.

Or why she would tell Dominga about it. Perhaps she thought it would help her sister get to class on time. Surely she never expected that Dalia and Dominga would use the map in one of their schemes. But then, villains are highly unpredictable.

Pausing outside the Emerald suite, Dalia looks right and left before hurrying across the hallway carpet. It is woven to look like a pond with gentle waves that ripple under her footsteps. At the end of the hall, she stops face-to-face with an ancient portrait of Princesa Viridiana, the most famous graduate of Casita Emerald. It is said that she planted the pine forest that surrounds the palace.

Dalia checks once again to be sure no one is watching. Then she curtsies in front of the portrait, as politely as she imagines a princesa would, before nudging the frame aside to reveal a hidden passage. She hoists herself into the small, dark space and crawls until she reaches a fork in the tunnel.

She reaches up and pushes hard on the loose plank above her head. Once she jostles it free, she stands, slowly and cautiously, emerging inside a grandfather clock. She dodges the swinging pendulum, whispers hello to the spiders that have spun their webs there, then clambers out the center door and races down yet another hallway until the toasty-sweet smell of burnt sugar tells her she is near.

Dalia crouches behind a pink sandstone sculpture of a mermaid and hisses. It is turkey vulture for "Are you there?" Dalia is an expert at animal-speak.

For several moments, there is only silence. Dalia takes a deep breath, preparing to hiss again. But then she hears a reply.

"Finally," Dominga whistles back. "I was beginning to worry you'd been caught."

Moments later, Dominga darts around the corner and down the hallway. Her tiara, silver and scattered with small round opals that look like bubbles in a potion bottle, is covered in flour. The edge of her apron is charred black, matching the gown underneath.

A smell, like campfire and honey, hovers around her.

Dalia sniffs. "A new dessert?"

Dominga takes off her glasses and wipes them with the edge of her apron. "Not dessert," she whispers. "It's the secret recipe I've been telling you about. It's going to get us into the B.A.D., I just know it, and—"

Dalia coughs. She hates to interrupt, but Dominga has a habit of getting ahead of herself, and their latest scheme requires terribly precise timing.

"Oh!" Dominga says. "We had better get going,

hadn't we?" She unties her apron and flings it around the mermaid's neck.

Then, together, Dalia and Dominga dash to the Great Hall.

They have been plotting all week. They must get there *after* the banquet tables have been set for dinner but *before* the princesas arrive to eat. It is an awfully small slice of time.

But they have planned everything perfectly. The hall is deserted. Their boots thud dully on the gleaming checkerboard floor. Cloth napkins, in the colors of each Casita, are folded into rose shapes on the tables. Empty plates, soon to be filled with buttery empanadas and creamy egg custard, rest between gleaming gold forks and spoons. Paper banners with flowers cut into them flutter from the rafters, and lanterns filled with flickering candles give the room a soft, shimmering glow.

"Did you send the invitations?" Dominga asks, grabbing one of the two long window hooks that hang on the wall.

"Naturally," Dalia says, taking the other. "And our guests are frightfully pleased to join us. What about you? Are you prepared to spread the word?"

Dominga raises her hook and uses it to unlatch one of the high windows that line the hall. The window falls open a crack, and she moves on to the next one. "I've been practicing every night," she says.

Dalia hopes it is enough. Dominga is newer to animal-speak than she is. She begins unhitching the windows on the opposite side of the room. They have only minutes now to finish their preparations with enough time to hurry back to the Casitas and fall into the dinner line behind the unsuspecting princesas.

Dalia imagines what will happen after that. The princesas will sit down to eat as usual. Once everyone is settled and dishes are being passed, Dalia will give a signal—a squeak so thin and high-pitched the princesas won't notice it.

But the bats will.

They will swoop in through the open windows to feast on strawberries and melon and pineapple from one of Chef Luís-Esteban's fruit towers. The beating of hundreds of wings will snuff out all the candles.

Then, in the panicked darkness, Dominga will summon the rest of their guests. Rats. To scurry over satin-slippered toes. To wriggle under the linen tablecloths.

Dalia shivers in anticipation. The screams alone will secure their spots at the B.A.D. She is sure of it. Maybe the villains of the B.A.D. will even be able to hear the terrified cries from their tower.

She opens the last window.

"The element of surprise is everything," she says. "We must get back to our Casitas."

CHAPTER 3

Dalia and Dominga scramble through the secret passageway and back to the Casitas as the dinner bells begin to ring. They split up at the corridor where Emerald's green carpet blurs into Opal's, which is woven to look like cottony clouds on a sun-soaked morning.

"Until later," Dominga screeches in turkey vulture.

"Wait for my signal," Dalia hisses back.

Dalia makes her way to the suite just in time to join the princesas on their way to the hall.

"Where were you?" Eloísa whispers. A fresh silk bow, brown this time to hide any spilled chocolate, bobs at her neck. She reaches to flick a cobweb off Dalia's tiara. "We thought you were going to be late again. Last time, I had to tell Profesora Colibrí that you got stuck feeding those frogs that are always hopping after you."

"Thanks," Dalia manages to croak, her voice thick with unexpected regret that she must lie to Eloísa. For a princesa, she's not *too* awfully annoying. *But villains must make difficult decisions*, she tells herself. *Villains must stop at nothing.*

Dalia's footsteps fall into rhythm with Eloísa's as they snake into the Great Hall. She looks for Dominga across the room and finds her, as usual, next to Princesa Inés.

Inés's red ringlets spill like a drizzle of strawberry sauce over the shoulders of her daffodil gown. Inés is determined to be named the Fairest of the F.A.I.R. someday. She is convinced that Dominga could tell her all Paloma's secrets if she wanted to. (Which she doesn't.)

Inés links arms with Dominga and pulls her toward the center of the Opal table. Dominga looks back at Dalia and rolls her eyes.

Dalia snickers to herself and walks toward her usual seat in the corner. But as she is about to sit down, she hears her name.

She turns in the direction of the sound and sees Eloísa waving. "Dalia!" she says. "Over here. Sit with us."

Dalia hesitates. She glances up at the windows that soon, if all goes according to plan, will fill with bats.

She'd better sit with the princesas, she decides. To keep them from becoming suspicious. She squeezes in between Eloísa and Carmen.

Soon, the hall fills with the cheerful buzz of royal chatter. A terribly tiresome sound, if you ask Dalia. She leans back while Carmen reaches over her to pluck a cube of pineapple off the fruit tower.

At the front of the room, the teachers sit at their own long table. Profesora Colibrí, perched at the center of them, flutters a fan in front of her long, thin nose.

"Any moment now," Dalia mutters.

Eloísa whips her head around. "What was that?"

Dalia gulps. "Any . . . more of the pumpkin empanadas?" she sputters. "Those are my favorite."

"I think so!" Eloísa chirps, and passes her the tray.

Dalia, her eyes still on the window, takes an empanada off the top. She lifts it to her mouth but freezes when she hears a small, high-pitched squeak. None of the princesas seem to notice it. And if they do, they might mistake it for the scrape of chair legs against the polished floors. Or a politely petite sneeze that was held in too long.

But Dalia recognizes it for what it is. Bat-speak for "Has the party started yet?"

Eloísa is scooping up a spoonful of custard. Carmen is laughing into her pale green goblet. No one is paying attention. The timing is perfect.

Dalia covers her mouth with her napkin and squeaks back. "Yes!" she replies in bat-speak. "We're ready for you!"

Nothing happens for a moment, and Dalia wonders whether she was loud enough. She sneaks a glance at Dominga and sees her staring at the windows while Inés babbles on.

Then, suddenly, the windows darken. A strange, low rustling spills into the hall.

Princesa Leonor pushes her wheelchair away from the Opal table and points. "What's that?"

Dalia and Dominga turn to each other across the room and mouth the word together: *bats*.

An instant later, hundreds of bats swoop through the unlatched windows, flapping and chirping.

It's working, Dalia thinks.

Dominga jumps to her feet. "It's working!" she shouts.

Dalia narrows her eyes, willing Dominga to keep quiet. It's too soon for celebration. The plan has only just begun.

But it doesn't matter. No one is listening to Dominga anyway. Glasses spill. Plates clatter.

"Hide!" Inés shrieks. She yanks a silver platter of empanadas off her table, dumps the flaky turnovers off, and holds it over her head.

Profesora Colibrí leaps from her seat. She hitches up her shimmering green-and-lavender skirt and runs to the center of the room, fan waving. But there's nothing she can do. There are too many bats. Their flapping wings blow out the lanterns, and the dining hall goes dark.

Next to Dalia, Eloísa screams. She grabs hold of the ragged edge of Dalia's gown and tugs. "Get down!" she says. "Take cover!"

Before she allows herself to be pulled under the table, Dalia hisses. "Now!" she calls out to Dominga in vulture-speak. "Do it now!"

Then, as Carmen's goblet of mint-and-cucumber

water spills over Dalia's head, she hears a quiet rumble, almost like a purr. "Come in," it says. "Join the feast!"

Dalia springs to her feet again. "No! That's not—" she starts to say.

But it's too late.

CHAPTER 4

"I just felt something!" Eloísa shouts. Her voice drops. "It was . . . kind of . . . soft, actually?"

"Me too," Carmen says. "Something cuddly."

"Whatever it is, get it away from me!" Inés wails.

Dalia slumps onto her seat, all the thrill of a perfect plot draining from her as the candles twinkle back to life.

"That's better," Profesora Colibrí says, nodding approvingly at the lanterns. Next, she flutters her fan, and a glittery yellow mist swirls around her. She waves a hand, and the mist drifts out the windows, leading the bats away with it.

Dalia surveys the Great Hall. Instead of rats nibbling off porcelain plates and stealing bits of lace for their nests, there are bunnies.

Dozens of them.

Fluffy and plump. Lops and cottontails. "I think I'll call mine Doña Kettlecorn," Eloísa says, climbing back into her chair and cradling a silky bunny with fur the color of buttered toast.

Dominga tiptoes toward Dalia, stepping gingerly over the bunnies—white and gray, brown and black—that pour in through crevices in the walls, noses twitching. "What went wrong?"

"Rat-speak can sound a lot like *rabbit*-speak." Dalia tries to hide the disappointment in her voice.

Dominga's glasses slide down her nose. "Oh," she says dully. "Of course."

"Anyone could have made the same mistake," Dalia replies. Although *she* wouldn't have.

On the other side of the room, Inés sneezes. "Get these filthy creatures out of here!" she says. "I am *allergic!*" She sneezes again, a blast that shakes a perfect curl out from under her tiara.

"Did you see that?" Dominga lifts her head. Her eyes twinkle. "We've made her sneeze. That must count for something."

Perhaps, Dalia thinks. *But a sneeze is not a scheme.*

"Atención, princesas!" Profesora Colibrí trills.

"Your delightful rabbit guests may stay, but it's time to set things back to order."

At that, the princesas work together the way princesas seem to *always* work together. Princesa Leonor rearranges the empanadas that Inés spilled as Princesa Jacinta sweeps up the crumbs. Eloísa hums while she and Carmen take hold of either end of the Emerald dining table and straighten it, careful not to step on any of the bunnies that hop in circles around their ankles. The whole scene is painfully pleasant.

"Be patient, Doña Kettlecorn." Eloísa giggles as the cream-and-brown ball of fluff darts between her feet. "Once I'm finished I can hold you again."

Inés sits, her feet raised on an overturned chair. She dabs her forehead with one of the last clean white Opal napkins. "I *would* help," she whimpers. "But all this commotion has given me a headache."

No more than a few minutes have passed, and already it is as if Dalia and Dominga's scheme had never happened at all.

Except for the rabbits, of course.

Profesora Colibrí observes from the center of the room, fluttering her fan in front of her nose. When the worst of the messes are tidied and the tables and chairs stand once again in neat rows, she snaps the fan shut. The princesas raise their heads.

"Much better." She nods. "Now, please take your seats, princesas. You may finish your dinner while I make an important announcement. I think you will find that this"—she pauses to shoo away a chocolate-colored bunny that's munching the edge of her skirt—"most curious visit from our woodland friends is not the only exciting event the evening has in store." Her black eyes sparkle. "Nor is it even the *most* exciting."

An eager murmur rises as the princesas settle back in to listen. Dalia and Dominga retreat to a shadowy corner of the hall, the only place the glow of the candles doesn't quite reach. Dalia has lost her appetite anyway. She and Dominga sink to the ground and rest their chins on their knees.

"What now?" Dominga asks. "I suppose we should write to the B.A.D. anyway," she continues, answering her own question. She pushes her glasses farther up her nose. "They might appreciate the *spirit* of the scheme. Our *ideas* are very villainous, after all."

Dalia thinks about those letters folded inside her geography book. All those rejections. She can't bear to receive another. "An idea is not enough," she replies. "We need a *perfect* plot." She presses her palms against the floor and feels the cool tile through the holes in her satin gloves.

A black rabbit with a patch of white fur around one eye hops toward them.

"Go away," Dalia says, more gruffly than she means to. The rabbit doesn't budge, though. He twitches his nose at her.

Dominga tries rabbit-speak. "Find someone else," she chirps. "We don't have any food for you."

"And we're not the cuddling types," Dalia adds.

The rabbit nuzzles against Dalia's lap and snuggles into the folds of her dreary gray gown. She yanks off her gloves and runs a hand over his head. It is terribly soft.

Profesora Colibrí has climbed on top of a table. Her hair glimmers blue and then violet under the chandeliers.

"Those of you whose family members are graduates of the F.A.I.R. will have heard of the Starlight Search," she is saying.

Oh no. Dalia flinches. The Starlight Search sounds obnoxiously nice. As usual.

"Ooh!" Inés jumps up, headache vanishing as if by magic. "The Starlight Search is one of the F.A.I.R.'s most treasured traditions," she blurts. "It's when—"

"Yes, gracias, Princesa," Profesora Colibrí says over her. Dalia might be imagining it, but Profesora Colibrí's smile seems to go stiff for a moment.

37

Inés curtsies and sits down again. "Of course *I* know all about—"

"As I was saying," Profesora Colibrí continues, "the Starlight Search is held every year on the night of the Cloudberry Moon. Profesora Astra has finished her calculations. It will be tonight."

She gestures toward one of the instructors, a tall woman with caramel-colored twists. She wears a midnight blue cape covered in swirling galaxies.

The princesas begin to whisper. Even Dominga leans forward. "Paloma wrote about this in one of her letters," she murmurs.

Dalia scratches between the rabbit's ears, pretending not to care.

"The Starlight Search is an opportunity for first-year princesas to demonstrate their courage and clever thinking as they get to know the palace," Profesora Colibrí explains. "Starting when the clock strikes midnight—and not a moment before—you will search for clues hidden throughout the grounds. The first team to reach the final destination will earn ten gems for their Casita's chalice."

The princesas cheer as Profesora Colibrí waves her fan toward the head of the room, where four golden cups, each as tall as she is, stand side by side. The Casitas earn a gem for every royal deed accomplished. The team with the most gems at the end of the term will win the privilege of leaving the palace grounds to explore the surrounding village.

Dominga whispers, "You know what this means, right?"

Dalia shakes her head. A stray curl bounces over her eyes. "More royal rubbish?" she grumbles.

Dominga nudges her. "No! Just think, with everyone on the hunt, we'll have the perfect chance to sneak out of the palace. We can be at the B.A.D. by this time tomorrow. I can already picture it! The spells! The schemes!" By the time she is finished, she is standing.

"Shh," Dalia hushes her. Profesora Colibrí has turned toward them and raised an eyebrow.

Dominga sits back down. Her gown billows up around her in a puff of black tulle. "Oh," she says. "Was I getting ahead of myself?"

She was. Again.

But Dalia doesn't tell her this. Instead, she explains what should be obvious. "Even if we manage to escape, what will we tell the B.A.D.

once we get there? Not a single one of our plots has gone according to plan."

Dominga's forehead crinkles. She digs her spell book from her pocket, opens it to a fresh page, and pulls a pencil out of her tangled bun. "What if we try again on our way out? We could spoil the Starlight Search, get all the princesas lost. While we're on our way to the B.A.D., they'll be stuck here. *Trapped!*"

Dalia imagines the scurry of silk slippers wandering in hopeless circles around the dark palace. Running into spiderwebs. Tripping over rats. Real rats this time.

It would be horrendous.

If they can pull it off.

The black bunny rubs his chin against Dalia's arm.

She's not sure they *can* pull it off, not after what just happened.

Profesora Colibrí raises her voice. "The honor of reading the first clue always goes to a princesa who embodies the spirit of cooperation and teamwork and fair play—so important to tonight's challenge."

Across the room, Inés sits up straighter. She pats her hair to make sure not a single ringlet is out of place. She scoots to the edge of her seat, ready to stand.

"This year," Profesora Colibrí says, "I would like to recognize *two* princesas."

Inés frowns, but she does not sit back.

"Dalia and Dominga," Profesora Colibrí announces. "See the way they have crossed the lines of their Casitas to work together in *true* princesa style."

She flutters her fan toward them. The princesas turn their heads and begin to applaud. Except Inés, who crosses her arms over her chest and looks away.

Dominga's mouth has fallen open.

Dalia's cheeks burn.

"Please come forward, princesas," Profesora Colibrí trills. "We're all waiting to hear the clue."

Gently, Dalia nudges the bunny off her gown. She and Dominga rise. There is no escaping it. As they trudge toward the center of the room, everyone still clapping, Dalia leans her head toward Dominga and mutters, "We're doing it. We're sabotaging the Starlight Search."

Profesora Colibrí gestures for them to join her on top of the table. Dominga goes first, then helps Dalia up. The profesora hands them a scroll, wrapped tightly with pink ribbon. Dalia and Dominga unwind the scroll. They clear their throats, and together, they read:

"*True princesas, take note: The key to every noble quest is to first seek harmony.*"

But harmony is the last thing on their minds.

CHAPTER
5

Señor De La Rosa escorts the bunnies back to the meadow, promising nibbles of cabbages and carrots from the palace vegetable garden along the way. When the last of them has hopped through the hall's giant oak doors, Profesora Colibrí addresses the princesas.

"I know it will be difficult to sleep after this evening's many surprises," she says. "But return to your rooms and try. The Starlight Search will commence when the clock strikes midnight."

Chairs scrape the floor as the princesas push back from the long dining tables. They whisper over the first clue.

"Finally," Dalia says. "We can get out of here." She and Dominga must think of a way to spoil the Starlight Search, and they have only until the end of the hallway to do it.

Dominga opens her spell book with its red leather cover and gold-edged pages. "We could jam the doors to all the suites," she suggests. "Trap the princesas before they even set out."

It would be terribly easy, Dalia thinks. They wouldn't need anything more than Dominga's hairpins to pull it off. But perhaps it is a bit *too* easy.

"Someone will come to free the princesas—someone *always* does—and then they'll simply get on with the search. No, we need to think of something positively putrid." She twists a curl that has fallen over her shoulder. "We could find the last clue and leave a surprise there. Something good."

And by good, she means very, very bad.

"Like skunk spray!" Dalia goes on. Her pace quickens as excitement builds. But then she stops so suddenly that Dominga, hurrying to catch up, nearly crashes into her. "Only I haven't seen any skunk tracks around the palace grounds. Perhaps you could cook up something in the kitchen that smells just as horrid."

Dominga wrinkles her nose as if she can almost smell it. "Perhaps," she says as they begin to walk again. "I'm not sure there's time. *But* suppose they never find the last clue at all? Suppose we steal the real clues and send the princesas someplace *else*."

Dalia opens her mouth to object, expecting to find some small detail that Dominga, in her eagerness, has overlooked. But she cannot. The plan is excellently evil.

"Someplace hidden," she adds instead.

"Someplace terrifying," Dominga agrees. "High in the clock tower, for example."

Someone screeches Dominga's name. For a moment, Dalia wonders if she is imagining the princesa's panicked shrieks. But the sound is real. It is coming, as usual, from Inés.

"Domingaaaaaaaa!" she hollers again.

Dominga ducks as Inés stands on tiptoe to scan the crowd for her. She won't be hard to spot. The dark gowns that she and Dalia wear stand out like wilted blooms in a spring bouquet.

"Where are you?" Inés asks, voice still raised. "I'm beginning to wonder if you even *want* Casita Opal to win."

Dominga keeps her chin dipped against her chest. Her glasses slide down her nose. "We'll have to stay ahead of Inés," she mumbles. "Otherwise, it'll never work."

Dominga is right. Inés will do anything to prove she deserves to be Fairest of the F.A.I.R., starting with winning the search.

Dalia has an idea. "Meet me outside the chicken coop in three hours," she says. "Everyone should be asleep by then. Bring your stockings."

They have arrived at the end of the corridor, where hallways leading to each Casita—Opal,

Emerald, Ruby, and Sapphire—branch out in four directions.

"There you are!" Inés says, striding toward them. "What are you doing with *her*?" She sneers at Dalia.

"It doesn't matter," Inés continues, not waiting for an answer. "We don't have time for your excuses. I need to fill you in on the plan." She leads Dominga away by the elbow.

Dominga looks over her shoulder and winks at Dalia. *Three hours*, Dalia mouths back, then darts down the Emerald hallway.

An hour before midnight, Dalia and Dominga stand outside Casita Opal, looking up. In their arms, they clutch their extra stockings, filled to bursting with feathers from the chicken coop.

50

"You remembered to unlatch it?" Dalia asks, nodding her chin at the window.

"Of course," Dominga answers.

"I still think you should have left the toad behind," Dalia says.

"And let her get eaten by the chickens?" Dominga replies. "Never!" She pats her pocket. "You'll see. She won't be any trouble at all."

"For the last time, the chickens wouldn't have eaten her," Dalia mumbles.

But Dominga isn't listening. With her stockings clutched in one arm, she begins to climb the trellis, thick with night-blooming jasmine. A feather falls from one of her stockings and drifts down onto Dalia's nose.

It tickles. Dalia feels a sneeze coming. She holds her breath and squinches her eyes shut to stifle it. She and Dominga must be silent. They can't risk waking the princesas. When Dalia is sure the sneeze has passed, she opens her eyes, sniffles, and starts to climb.

Dominga reaches the window and pushes it gently. It creaks as it opens. Dalia cringes at the sound.

Carefully, Dominga peeks inside. "Don't worry," she chatters down in squirrel-speak. "They're still asleep." She crawls through.

Dalia lets out her breath and follows.

Once they're both inside, Dominga moves to pull the window shut behind them. But Dalia reaches out to stop her. "Better not," she whispers. "In case it creaks again." They can't take any more chances.

Stepping lightly in the dark, they make their way to the door. They kneel and begin to stuff their feather-filled stockings into the gap above the floorboards, hoping to muffle the outside noise so that the Opal princesas sleep through the midnight chimes. That should slow Inés down long enough for Dalia and Dominga to find the clues and replace them.

When they have finished, Dominga looks at Dalia and points toward the window. *Shall we leave?* she seems to be asking.

But Dalia shakes her head. She holds up a finger and beckons. *Not yet*, she says without a word. *Follow me.*

Inés sleeps under a pink canopy with constellations stitched into it in sparkling golden thread. Her red hair is coiled into tight pin curls. Dalia tiptoes toward her.

She peels off her gloves and stuffs them with

extra feathers. If they can somehow slip the gloves between Inés's ears and the ribbons that fasten her silk sleep mask, they can be all the more certain she won't hear the midnight chimes. Dalia holds the gloves up to her own ears, miming her plan to Dominga.

Dominga nods. Dalia passes her one of the gloves, and they creep up on either side of Inés. Moving as slowly and silently as possible, Dalia reaches for the ribbon. Her fingertips are nearly touching it when a loud "SQUAWK!" sends her scrambling backward.

"Aaah!" Dominga screams. She flings the glove, sending feathers flying across the room. Inés groans.

Dalia and Dominga look toward the window, where a black-and-white-speckled hen flaps her wings. "I knew it was you!" the bird clucks in chicken-speak. "You'd better have a very good reason for disturbing us in the middle of the night. And I hope you're not expecting eggs tomorrow."

Dalia and Dominga first met the hen when they wandered by accident into the coop on their second day at the F.A.I.R. Despite her complaints, she seems to have grown rather attached to Dominga.

"Shh!" Dalia tries to shush the bird. "Dominga, keep her quiet!" Still, she knows this is at least partly her fault. She should have let Dominga shut the window.

"If you could just wait for me outside," Dominga clucks back, stepping toward the window, "I won't be long."

It's hopeless. Even in the dim light, Dalia can see that the princesas are already stirring.

"Don't like me in your bedroom, eh?" the hen persists. "Well, how do you think we liked you in our coop? Stomping around in your boots, stealing our feathers *and* our toad. And such a tasty-looking one too."

Still tucked in Dominga's pocket, the toad croaks.

Leonor pulls her blanket up to her chin. "Dominga, is that you?" she asks. "Why are you *clucking*, and where did all these feathers come from?"

Without answering, Dominga leaps toward the window and scrambles out. "Let's go!" she calls out to Dalia.

Princesa Lizeth rolls over and stretches.

Dalia drops to the floor, preparing to crawl after Dominga. She reaches out with one hand and feels for the plush, pearl-white rug.

Then she squints as a candle appears suddenly in front of her face.

"Just what," Inés asks, her words clipped, "do you think you're doing here?"

CHAPTER 6

Inés stands, her back to the window. Dalia sits up on her knees and can just make out Dominga's fingers, clinging to the ledge. *Keep going,* she wishes she could tell her. *Get away while you can still save our scheme.*

But she doesn't dare.

"Well?" Inés asks, tapping the toe of her satin slipper. "Are you going to explain what you're doing in *our* suite?" Her hand is on her hip, wrinkling the ruffles on her pale yellow night-dress. She does not wait for Dalia to respond.

"I'll tell you what she's doing," Inés says, glancing around the room. Lizeth and Leonor are both sitting up in their beds now. "Spying."

She glares at Dalia. "You think you can win the Starlight Search by following us, don't you?" She smiles then. "I can't say I blame you when it's so obvious we're going to win. Still, I wonder what Profesora Colibrí would say." She shrugs. "Let's find out!" She walks toward the door.

"No, wait!"

If Inés calls the profesora now, the whole plot will unravel. Just like all the others.

Inés turns. Dalia looks around the rest of the room. Leonor rubs her eyes. Lizeth yawns. The hen, who caused this whole mess, settles on top of Dominga's pillow and clucks happily.

"That isn't why I'm here," Dalia says, her mind whirring. "I came to wake up Dominga. We... wanted a head start. It isn't midnight yet. If you leave Profesora Colibrí out of this, you could get a head start too."

Inés opens her mouth as if she's about to argue. Instead, she closes it again. "Of course we don't *need* a head start, but since we're all awake anyway, it couldn't hurt."

It's working. Dalia's shoulders relax. She and Dominga didn't slow Inés down the way they wanted to. But with Dominga's map of the palace—combined with their cunning—they still have a chance to get out ahead of her.

A croak comes from the window. "Good thinking," Dominga congratulates her in toad-speak.

Inés shivers. "Is that window open? I knew I felt a draft."

"I'll get it!" Dalia rushes to the window while Inés glides back to her bed. She begins removing pins from her hair. They plink as she drops them onto her nightstand. *Plink, plonk, plink.* She pauses, hands poised above the next curl. "What are you waiting for?" she shouts at Leonor and Lizeth. "Get going!"

Leonor and Lizeth look at each other. "But, Inés," Leonor says, "if we start the search now, before midnight, wouldn't we be *cheating*?"

Inés pulls out two more pins. "Of course not," she says. "Princesas should be prepared. Princesas should take advantage of every opportunity. You wouldn't want Profesora Colibrí to think we're lazy, would you?" She steps behind a dressing screen.

This is Dalia's chance. She swings one leg out the window. While Inés and the others are arguing, she and Dominga can sneak away.

"Not so fast!" Inés barks, her head peeking

out from behind the screen. "How do I know you aren't going to rush straight back to Casita Emerald and wake them up too? How do I know you aren't going to tell them all our plans?"

"Inés, I—" Dalia begins as she climbs back into the room.

"No!" Inés interrupts. "You're staying here with us." She ducks back behind the screen and emerges moments later in one of her dazzling yellow gowns, this one with a burst of silk buttercups at each shoulder. "You and Dominga." She takes a silver candlestick off her nightstand and waves it toward Dominga's bed.

It is empty. Except for the chicken.

"Where is she?" Lizeth asks, unwinding a silk scarf from around her curls. "I was sure I saw her just a moment ago."

"I still don't understand what all these feathers are for," Leonor murmurs, picking one off the sleeve of her lavender pajamas.

"She's already run off ahead of us, hasn't she?" Inés says. "Trying to get an unfair advantage." She marches toward the window.

Dalia shifts, trying to conceal Dominga from view. "Where's Dominga?" She stalls. "Well, she's . . . she's . . ."

"Here!" Dominga croaks in toad-speak as she drops something behind Dalia's back. "Tell her it's me."

"Huh?" Dalia reaches behind her and wraps her fingers around a brownish-greenish and slightly befuddled toad. She holds it in front of her and peers at it. Tied loosely around the toad's middle is a scrap of black lace, pulled from Dominga's gown. A pair of tiny glasses, made from a bent hairpin, rests over its eyes.

Dalia grins as her surprise melts into appreciation. "She's *right here*, as a matter of fact," she says finally. She presents the toad to Inés.

Inés scowls and shuffles backward. "What is *that*?"

"I told you," Dalia answers. "It's Dominga." She hears Dominga snort outside the window, and coughs to cover the sound. "She thought an enchantment would help with the search. As a, erm, *toad*, she can fit through crevices the rest of us can't."

Leonor, who has swiveled from her bed onto her wheelchair, hurries toward her. She lifts the toad out of Dalia's hands.

"She *does* seem to be wearing Dominga's gown," she says, then winks at Dalia.

Inés frowns. "You can't expect me to believe that *creature* is Dominga."

"It's just like in that fairy tale," Dalia insists. "The one where a witch turns the brothers into swans."

Lizeth climbs out of bed and hops behind her own dressing screen. She's tall enough that the top of her head peeks out above it. "That one's my favorite," she says.

Inés squints down at the toad, still unconvinced.

"Honestly, Inés, I can't believe you don't recognize an enchanted toad when you see one." Dalia shakes her head. "And you call yourself a true princesa."

Two pink blotches spread over Inés's cheeks like spilled cranberry juice. She tilts up her chin and sniffs. "It's just that I'm so shocked Dominga would attempt an enchantment. It's forbidden until our fourth year."

"I think Paloma taught her," Dalia says.

"Princesa Paloma?" Inés looks down at the toad again. "I see it now. Those are Dominga's eyes." She takes the toad from Leonor and drops it in her own pocket. "Better let me handle her."

Dalia hears another croak coming from outside the window, only fainter this time.

"I'm going to the kitchen for my secret recipe," Dominga says in toad-speak. "I'll catch up with you. The plot is still afoot!"

"I'll leave you a trail," Dalia croaks back. She hears no reply, only Dominga's footsteps scampering off into the night.

"What was that?" Inés demands. "Are you speaking to Dominga? Is it a secret code? What did you tell her? Answer me!"

"Only that she doesn't need to worry," Dalia replies. "Now that *you're* in charge."

Inés pats the toad's head, turns, and goes back to her nightstand. She lifts her tiara off its satin cushion and places it on her head. It glimmers in the candlelight.

"Everyone take a lantern," she says. "The Starlight Search starts now."

CHAPTER 7

While the princesas file out the door, Dalia lingers and swipes a stick of charcoal off the pile of art supplies on Leonor's nightstand. She puts it in her pocket.

"Let's go!" Inés growls. "You're costing us time."

"Of course," Dalia says. "I'm coming." She has made a very quick calculation.

Dalia never asked to be on this team. But if she helps the princesas find the next clue before the others do, she might still be able to swap it for a phony one, ditch Inés, and find Dominga. It won't be easy. Then again, perhaps the B.A.D. will appreciate the challenge.

They *have* to.

"The first clue was about notes, wasn't it?" Lizeth asks when Dalia closes the door. "I wonder if the next one is in a classroom."

"But there was also something about a *key*," Leonor says, raking her fingers through her auburn hair, still sleep-tangled. "I think we should start at the guardhouse."

Inés turns and stares at Dalia. "And I suppose *you* probably think you know where it is?"

Dalia hesitates. Words seem to stick to the top of her mouth. Actually helping the princesas is harder than she thought it would be, especially when it would be so easy to send them off in the wrong direction. But she must resist. For the good of the scheme.

"It's the music salon," she forces herself to say. "I think the clue meant *musical* notes and *musical* keys. And—"

"Harmony," Inés interrupts. "Precisely. We'll find the clue in the music salon. That's exactly what I was about to say." The toad peeks out over the side of her pocket, and she pushes its head back down before striding ahead.

"Get a move on!" she calls over her shoulder. "But be quiet. We don't want to get caught . . . er . . . I mean . . ." She pauses midstep and shakes her head. Her curls bounce over her shoulder. "I mean . . . unlike *some* people around here, I wouldn't want to disturb anyone's sleep."

Leonor sighs and moves forward after Inés. Lizeth follows, and Dalia takes her place at the end. They creep down the hall, across the Opal carpet. As they move over it, its woven clouds seem to part and drift, revealing a glimpse of a rainbow, just visible in the lantern light.

Dalia keeps her eyes on those clouds, trying not to think about the stack of rejection letters back in her room. She cringes when she imagines what the director of the B.A.D. would think if she saw her in line with these princesas. Not foiling them. Not fooling them. But *following* them. As if she were one of them.

She slows her steps.

But then, as if sensing Dalia falling behind, Inés stops. She stomps her foot. A billowy cumulus cloud breaks apart under her heel.

"Dalia," she orders without looking back, "get up here."

Dalia raises her head. Inés has come to a place

where the hallway splits. They can continue to follow the Opal carpet or veer left, through another even darker and narrower corridor.

"Don't you know where you're going?" Dalia asks.

"Of course I know where I'm going," Inés says. "I just don't want you to get lost."

"In that case, maybe we should split up," Dalia suggests. "To see which way is the fastest." Dalia's heartbeat speeds. This could be her chance to ditch the princesas. She points down the Opal walkway. "You all stay on this path while I—"

Leonor moves forward and stops beside Inés. "No, that way's fastest," she interrupts, raising her lantern toward the darker hallway. "It leads to the art studio, and the music salon must be nearby. I can hear the piano lessons when I'm cleaning my brushes."

Inés scowls at Dalia, then peers into the darkness. She tugs the edge of one of her gloves. "Are you *sure*?" she asks.

"You're not afraid, are you?" Lizeth asks.

Dalia steps backward. She could still get away. She just needs an excuse.

She croaks, "How would you like some earthworms?"

"I'm listening," the toad answers, its croak muffled by the heavy silk of Inés's gown.

"Quiet, Dominga," Inés says, patting her pocket. "I'm trying to think."

"I'll give you five of them," Dalia croaks again. "Freshly dug from the mud by the pond."

The toad sticks her head out of Inés's pocket.

"The ones by the pond?" the toad asks. "What's the catch?"

Dalia smiles to herself. She's never met a toad who could resist earthworms. "Hardly anything at all," Dalia says. "Just jump out of that pocket and keep going, back the way we came."

She'll offer to chase the toad—Inés won't want to leave the search—and race back to the Opal suite. Once there, she'll climb out the window and catch up with Dominga. With Paloma's map, they can still beat the princesas to the salon.

"You can even take off that ridiculous outfit," Dalia adds.

The toad tips her head and looks down at the scrap of black lace covering her belly. "I think it suits me. And anyway, I was starting to get comfortable in here." She burrows back into the pocket.

"*Ten* worms!" Dalia blurts.

"Make it fifteen," the toad replies.

Inés's gaze snaps to Dalia and then to her pocket.

"What was that?" she demands. "You two aren't up to something, are you?"

Leonor swivels and moves closer to Dalia. Lizeth turns and stares.

"No!" Dalia says. "Of course not. I was merely asking Dominga if *she* knows the quickest way to the music salon. Since her sister was a student here."

Inés scowls. "Of course. Why didn't you say something before?" She opens her pocket. She reaches for the toad.

"Fifteen!" Dalia croaks. "Go! Now!"

Just before Inés's fingers close around her, the toad leaps from her pocket. "I'll be waiting for those earthworms," she says before bounding down the hall.

"Get back here!" Inés shrieks. "Where are you going? That's the wrong way!"

The toad doesn't stop.

Dalia starts after her. "Don't worry!" she says. "I'll catch her. You three go on ahead."

"Finally," Leonor says. She and Lizeth maneuver around Inés and make their way down the dark hallway. Soon, their flickering lantern lights are all Dalia can make out of them.

"Go!" Dalia urges Inés. "You don't want them to find the clue without you."

Still, Inés hesitates. She looks once more down the shadowy hallway.

"No," she says. "I'll go after Dominga. She's heading back to the Opal dormitory, and we don't want you snooping around." She grins. "Don't worry. With Dominga's shortcuts, I'm sure we'll catch up to you. Or who knows? Maybe we'll get there first."

She hitches up her gown and tears down the hall, bumping Dalia's shoulder as she passes.

Leonor's voice floats in from the opposite direction. "Aren't you coming?"

Dalia groans. "Be right there."

She takes the charcoal from her pocket and draws a tiny bat on the wall. This way, if Dalia can't find Dominga, maybe Dominga can still find her.

CHAPTER 8

Back in the Emerald suite, Eloísa's eyes pop open. She fell asleep puzzling over the first clue. And somehow, in her dreams, the answer came to her, as clear as a melody she had known her whole life.

True princesas, take note: The key to every noble quest is to first seek harmony.

She sits straight up. It's the music salon, of course. She should have guessed it from the start.

She has spent so many hours there strumming the guitar, plucking the harp, playing the violin. Better yet, she could find the music room in her sleep.

Then she turns to the window. The Cloudberry Moon gleams bright in an inky-blue sky. The chimes still haven't rung. She must wait. But there's no way she can get back to sleep now.

She lights the candle on her nightstand. She scrambles out of her pajamas and into a fresh pair of satin pants, these ones with silver music notes stitched down each leg. She takes a matching cape from her wardrobe and drapes it over her shoulders. In the mirror, she practices swishing it the way she will when she leads her team to victory.

Then she flops back down on her bed. Now what?

She taps her foot against the bed frame in rhythm with Carmen's soft snore. The crickets outside chirp a thin, spooky melody, interrupted every now and then by an owl's distant hoot.

Eloísa knows she should let the rest of her roommates sleep. They have a long night of searching ahead of them. But she is bursting with this discovery and isn't sure how much longer she can wait to share it. It feels the same as when she has a new song in her mind and can't help but sing it, even when Maestra Allegra, the music instructor, insists that she pay attention to the notes on the page and not the ones in her head.

But if she were to *accidentally* wake up Dalia, whose bed is nearest hers, no one could get very upset, could they? She nudges a harmonica off her nightstand. It lands on the floor with a thunk.

She glances over at Dalia's bed. Dalia doesn't move.

"Hmm." Eloísa gets up. She walks over for a closer look.

Dalia doesn't move because Dalia isn't there! Eloísa pulls aside Dalia's quilt, a patchwork of black and purple and silver squares, to find only a pillow and a jumble of gray gowns where Dalia ought to be.

Eloísa checks under the bed and then inside Dalia's wardrobe. Both empty.

"She's gone!" Eloísa yells, no longer concerned about keeping quiet. A cool breeze ruffles the silk tie at her neck. Eloísa looks up and notices for the first time that their bedroom window is cracked open.

Carmen sits up straight. "Is it time for practice?

I'll be ready in two minutes." She pulls her dark blonde hair into a messy ponytail.

Marisol rolls over and pulls her velvety bedspread over her face. "Just a little while longer, okay?"

Eloísa lights the candlesticks on each princesa's nightstand so that the room fills with a golden glow. She dashes over to Marisol's bed and yanks away the banket.

"It's not okay," she says. "We have to find her. We have to go now!" Eloísa has been trying to ask Dalia to teach her some of those birdcalls she is so good at. It's for a woodland symphony Eloísa is composing. But every time she tries, Dalia finds a way to disappear.

Dalia must be quite shy, Eloísa has decided. She doesn't seem to have made many friends here. The Starlight Search would have been the perfect time to get to know each other—but not if Dalia is already gone.

The palace clock begins to chime midnight. Eloísa pauses and listens to each deep and dreamy clang. Then she hears the gentle thud of footsteps coming from nearby rooms as the other princesas awaken and prepare for the search. She imagines them whispering over the first clue, planning the paths they will take.

Her own team must move quickly if they want to find Dalia and join the search in time to win.

Carmen tightens the laces of her leather boots and pulls a pair of fern-green gloves over her hands. Then she places her tiara on top of her head. "Those were the chimes," she says, walking over to jostle Marisol's shoulder. "We need to get going. Emerald is tied with Opal. If we're the first team to solve all the clues, we'll be ahead by ten gems."

Eloísa wishes she had a conductor's baton so she could tell these two princesas what she needs them to do. Instead, she stands in the middle of the room and claps her hands until she has their attention.

"We'll be the first team," she says. "But first, we need to find Dalia."

Carmen and Marisol turn toward Dalia's bed. The canopy, spiderwebs strung across its edges, hangs over an empty mattress. Dalia's books are stacked on her nightstand next to a small black stone that shines like glass. Her tiara is gone.

"She could be anywhere," Carmen says, frowning. "Searching for Dalia will only slow us down. I'm sure she wouldn't want us to lose because of her."

Marisol, wide-awake now, ties a sash around her mint-green gown. "Besides," she says, "Dalia *likes* to be alone. And don't you think she's a little bit . . . *different*? With the webs and the black wardrobe?"

"Not to mention the lizard thing," Carmen adds.

They have a point. Dalia seems to think the lizard she carries around in her boot is a secret. But you can't exactly ignore its tail hanging at her ankle like an extra shoelace. Much less the way Dalia whispers to it when she thinks no one is watching.

Still, Eloísa can remember when people thought *she* was different because the music that played in her head sometimes carried her away until she forgot all about the world around her. Yet, it was that same music that Profesora Colibrí said had earned her a spot at the F.A.I.R.

Dalia is a bit strange. That is true. Then again, a bassoon is a bit strange too, with a skinny silver tube jutting out of it like a goose's neck. But the orchestra wouldn't sound the same without it.

Eloísa looks up at the green pennants strung across Carmen's bedposts and at the tennis racket leaning against her nightstand. "But Dalia is part of our *team*," she protests. "Profesora Colibrí wouldn't want us to leave her behind. Besides, she might need our help. And who knows? Maybe we need hers. Maybe we *need* someone a little bit different."

"Fine," Carmen relents. "We'll find Dalia and then we'll win the prize. Let's go."

CHAPTER 9

The music salon is usually alive with awfully cheerful sounds. Now, lit only by the light of their lanterns, the room seems almost haunted. The silent instruments look as if they are waiting for ghostly hands to play them. Dalia wishes Dominga were there to see it too. She draws another bat by the door, then follows Leonor and Lizeth inside.

Leonor moves close to the harp and runs her fingers across its strings. Lizeth goes to the shelves of sheet music and begins leafing through them to look for the next clue. Dalia creeps toward the black piano on the other side of the room. As she steps closer, it begins to play, the notes high and silvery like wind chimes in a breeze.

"What was that?" Lizeth asks, dropping an armful of music. The sheets flutter to the floor and settle around her feet.

Dalia's heart thuds. She nearly backs away from the enchanted piano until she reminds herself that even more fabulously frightening things await her at the B.A.D. She must get used to unexpected chills. She steps closer, and the music grows louder and deeper, almost thunderous.

"We were wrong. It's not in here," Leonor says,

her voice wavering. "Let's go. We'll search in the classrooms, just like Lizeth said."

Lizeth is already halfway back to the door.

But Dalia doesn't stop. When she's near enough to touch the keys, she notices a scroll on the music rack, tied with pink ribbon. The next clue.

She reaches for the scroll, and when her fingers grasp it, every note on the piano plays at once in one horrible, sour chord.

Lizeth covers her ears with her hands. Leonor yells, "Make it stop!"

Dalia hides the scroll underneath her cloak, and the notes begin to fade.

"Was that the clue?" Lizeth asks, drawing closer now. "What does it say?"

Dalia backs up into the piano. "It's nothing," she says. "Just a scrap." Somehow, she must get rid of these princesas and replace the clue with a fake one. "I think you were right all along. The clue isn't in here, it's—"

"Give me that!" Inés demands, striding toward her. Inés's tiara, usually perfectly perched atop her copper curls, is askew. She is holding the toad. The toad's makeshift glasses are bent, but she's still wearing that torn piece of Dominga's lace. "You're hiding something. Under your cloak. Give it to me."

Dalia narrows her eyes at the toad. She was supposed to hop *away*.

"It's not my fault," the toad croaks defensively. "She's faster than she looks when she's angry."

Dalia whips the scroll around behind her back. "I don't know what you're talking about."

Inés lunges. "That's the clue, isn't it? Give it here!"

Dalia raises the scroll high above her head, no longer worried that Leonor and Lizeth might see it. But that doesn't stop Inés from reaching yet again. Dalia twists. Inés stretches out her fingers. But instead of grabbing the scroll, she catches hold of Dalia's necklace and pulls.

The chain snaps. The necklace flies out of Inés's hand, slides across the floor, and comes to a stop under the windows, which are draped in heavy mauve curtains.

Dalia gasps and drops the scroll. She runs to retrieve the necklace.

Leonor, who is nearest the window, gets there first and picks it up off the ground. She opens the locket and gazes at the picture inside.

Dalia's eyes sting.

"It's beautiful," Leonor says, holding the necklace out to Dalia. "You should wear it more often."

Dalia wears it always, just not where anyone can see. She takes the still-open locket from Leonor's hands and stares at it. A woman's face stares back. She has crimson lips and shining black eyes and curls just like Dalia's, only hers are swept into a delicate lace net that looks like a spiderweb glistening in the moonlight.

Inés, holding the scroll, peers over Dalia's shoulder. "She looks familiar."

Dalia didn't hear her coming. She snaps the locket shut and shoves it into her pocket.

Inés shrugs, carries the scroll back to the piano bench, and sits.

"Who is it?" Leonor asks in a whisper, inching closer to Dalia. "The woman in the picture."

Dalia hesitates a moment, but why should she? The princesas won't recognize her. "My mother," she mumbles. What she does not mention is that her mother also happens to be the director of the B.A.D. The same school she has been trying desperately to get into. The same school that keeps telling her she's not dreadful enough to attend.

She lets her hair fall over her eyes while she tries to blink back her tears. With such a powerful villain for a mother, dreadfulness should come naturally. She cannot fail again.

Lizeth drums her fingers over the top of the piano. "I don't understand. I thought you said you *didn't* have the clue."

"Oh, don't blame Dalia for not noticing the clue when it was staring her in the face," Inés replies. She unties the ribbon. "She's not exactly princess material."

If only the B.A.D. could hear that, Dalia thinks.

Inés straightens and clears her throat.

Lizeth and Leonor gather closer. Dalia is about to join them when she hears a rustling behind the curtains.

She looks in the direction of the sound.

"I now present the next clue," Inés announces.

"Just read it already." Leonor groans.

"Fine," Inés says. "I thought I'd make it more *royal*, but that's something you obviously don't appreciate. Here's the next clue: *It is time to embark on the next chapter of your search, a place where fantastic journeys begin and end.*"

Dalia is hardly listening. That's because, in the shadows behind the curtains, she sees a boot. A black leather boot.

Dominga's black leather boot. Right where the locket fell.

Maybe none of the princesas would recognize Dalia's mother's face. But Dominga would.

Dalia whistles in bat-speak. "Let me explain."

"Dalia, are you even paying attention?"

In the moment it takes Dalia to turn toward Inés, Dominga slips out the window, leaving her spell book behind.

CHAPTER
10

Hidden inside the spell book's pages are the palace map as well as the notes Dominga has scribbled about their schemes so far. All their wicked ideas and terrifying tricks. The two of them had only just begun their careers as villains. Dalia's chest tightens as she thinks about the dreadful deeds they planned to accomplish together. About how angry Dominga had to have been to leave the book behind.

She bends to pick it up and puts it in her pocket, along with the necklace and the charcoal pencil. She should have told Dominga the truth before. But she was too embarrassed—with such an infamous villain for a mother, Dalia should have had no trouble getting into the B.A.D.

She had also been a little afraid. Dominga claimed to be a villain, and Dalia believed her.

Mostly.

Still, people tend to stop talking to Dalia once they find out who her mother is. Sometimes it's as if they stop even *seeing* her. And even though she tells everyone, including herself, that she prefers to be on her own, she doesn't always.

"I *allowed* you to come along with us because I thought you were going to *help*." Inés's voice slices through the stillness. "But if you're just going to stand there, I'll call Profesora Colibrí and turn the two of you in right now."

"Two of us?" Dalia asks. Her shoulders tense with worry that somehow Inés spotted Dominga too.

Inés points to the toad, returned to her pocket. The toad croaks.

"Oh." Dalia lets out her breath. "Right. Listen, you got your head start, and now you have the second clue. Why don't you let me and"—she has to pause and purse her lips to keep her mouth from twitching—"me and *Dominga* go? That way you can win on your own?"

If Inés lets her go, Dalia can find Dominga— the real Dominga—and try to explain. Or at least return the spell book.

Inés laughs. It is almost a cackle. Leonor shudders and steers herself away.

"You heard Profesora Colibrí," Inés says. "A true

princesa must be terribly clever, and you're not cleverer than I am. You two only want to sneak off to finish the search yourselves." She shakes her head. "That's not happening. Now, tell us the best way to get to the carriage house."

Dalia had hoped to trap all the princesas in the tower. But so far tonight, the only person she has managed to trap is herself.

"Why would you go to the carriage house?"

Inés rubs her temples. "Haven't you been listening *at all*? Leonor, tell her. I can't bear to repeat myself."

Leonor rests her chin in her hands, looking like she'd escape this search too if she had the chance. "Inés thinks the next clue is in the carriage house," she says.

Lizeth slaps her hands on her lap. "And *I* disagree," she says.

"For the last time," Inés says, "it's simple." She unrolls the scroll once more and repeats the clue.

"Tell them," Inés says. "Where else could it be but the carriage house? That's where we *embark*. That's where all our journeys begin *and* end. Including, I might add, the journey that brought us to the F.A.I.R. in the first place. It's *poetic*."

Lizeth springs up off the piano bench. Her gown, white with peach-colored flowers that trail down from the waist, sweeps the floor.

"But Profesora Colibrí wouldn't want us to disturb the horses," she argues. "Especially when they're resting."

With her fingernail, Leonor sketches a tiny rose into the dust on one of the music stands. "I'm with Lizeth," she says.

Inés crosses her arms over her chest. They all look at Dalia.

Inés is wrong, of course. If Dalia agrees with her, the princesas will end up stuck on the other side of the palace grounds. They'll lose so much time they might never be able to finish the search. It's a tempting idea.

Then again, Dalia would be stuck with them. And she wouldn't have trapped anyone in the clock tower like she and Dominga planned.

But if she can find the next clue—and manage to hang on to it this time—she'll have one more chance to swap it out and sabotage the search for *all* the princesas.

The B.A.D. will surely welcome her if she pulls it off. Her and Dominga both. And then Dominga will have to forgive her.

Won't she?

"It *could* be the carriage house," she says finally.

"Thank you," Inés says. "Now, if you two are

finished wasting our time, there's a search to get on with." She tosses her curls over one shoulder and marches toward the door.

Neither Lizeth nor Leonor follows.

"But I think it probably isn't," Dalia continues.

Inés turns so quickly the toad nearly tumbles out of her pocket. She croaks angrily.

"I'm sorry, Dominga," Inés scolds, "but you're not being any help at all, so I must ask you to keep quiet." She glares at Dalia. "If not the carriage house, then where do you suggest we look?"

Dalia glances from Leonor to Lizeth to Inés.

"The library," she answers.

Leonor's eyes widen in sudden understanding. Inés stares blankly back. "What does a *library* have to do with a *journey*?"

"A journey of the mind," Leonor says, tapping her temple. "Of the *imagination*."

"And you know what's filled with beginnings and endings?" Lizeth adds. "Books."

"And do you know what's filled with books?" Dalia asks.

"The library." Inés nods. "Exactly what I was thinking. Follow me!"

CHAPTER 11

They have not traveled far down the dreary, torch-lit hallway when Inés stops, grabs Dalia's wrist, and pulls her to the front of the line. "On second thought," she says, "you go first."

"I thought you wanted to lead the way," Dalia protests.

"Now I can keep my eye on both of you." Inés pats her pocket. The toad squirms.

Dalia smirks and continues walking. She doesn't mind. She never wanted to follow Inés in the first place. Outside, the Cloudberry Moon has risen high in the sky. Its pale blue glow shines through the hallway's narrow windows. It's so bright they almost don't need their lanterns. Bright enough that if Dalia were to stop and look out, she could probably find the spindly towers of the B.A.D. She tells herself her footsteps are taking her there as surely as they are taking her to the library. She tells herself she hasn't made a terrible mistake.

Dalia listens for the sounds of the other princesas catching up to them, and for Dominga's turkey vulture hiss. But all she can hear is the rustle of their skirts and then Lizeth's nervous whisper behind her.

"I don't remember the way to the library being so creepy," Lizeth says. "I definitely don't remember so many cobwebs."

Another web catches on Dalia's tiara. "This is the quickest way," she answers, keeping secret that it's a path she and Dominga discovered on Paloma's map. "Trust me." She tightens her cloak around her shoulders.

Moments later, Leonor squeals. "What's *that*?"

Dalia looks up. A shadow like a withered arm with jagged claws at the ends of its fingers trembles on the wall.

Inés ducks behind Dalia, clinging to her cloak. "This is all your fault!" she howls.

"There's nothing to worry about," Dalia says, shaking her cloak free from Inés's grasp. *Yet*, she adds in her head. She holds her lantern up to one of the windows. "It's just the moon shining on a tree branch," she explains, trying to make her voice as calm and soothing as her abuelos' voices had been when she was first getting used to the noises on their farm.

Mamá left her there after she'd received a letter, delivered by ravens, from the B.A.D. The letter that had invited her to become the academy's director.

If anyone had bothered to ask Dalia what she wanted, she would have told them she wanted to go along with Mamá. Think how advanced she would be if she had been studying with expert villains all these years instead of attempting to teach herself.

But maybe, even then, Mamá believed she was not villain material. Dalia would prove her wrong.

To cheer her up and introduce her to the children in their village, Abuela and Abuelo planned an enormous party. For a week, they prepared food and hung streamers. They even tidied the spare bedrooms so they would be ready for an impromptu sleepover.

They shouldn't have bothered. No one came.

Her abuelos tried to hide their worry, but Dalia saw the way they twisted their fingers into knots. The way they glanced hopefully over their shoulders at the path that led to their home, searching for party guests who would never arrive.

So, Dalia gathered all the party hats they had made and started putting them on the animals. The barn cat purred at her ankles. The pig grunted cheerfully. The horse whinnied. *They* all wanted to talk to her. They were the only friends she needed.

Until she made a new one.

"Did you hear me?" Inés's voice shakes Dalia back to the present. "I *said*, if you get us lost, that's it. I'm telling Profesora Colibrí everything, and the two of you will never be allowed into the palace again."

Dalia continues walking. "We're not lost," she says. "The library is right this way."

They come to a painting of a giant magnolia tree with branches that stretch wide against a midnight blue sky. Tiny lights twinkle in its leaves, and the smell of its blossoms sweetens the air. Dalia stands on tiptoe and taps the top right corner of the painting's silver frame.

The painting swings open like a door, and Dalia steps aside to let the rest of them through. Leonor runs her fingers over the brushstrokes as she passes. Once the three princesas have entered,

Dalia fishes the charcoal out of her pocket and draws another small bat on the wall beside the painting—just in case Dominga is still following. Then she pulls the door shut.

Leonor, Lizeth, and Inés stare in amazement at Dalia and, behind her, the wall they've just passed through. The edges of the door are already melting into the wallpaper, printed with wispy feathers that seem to tumble and flutter in an invisible breeze.

Books surround them, arranged not on shelves but in towers that swirl up from the floor and arches that sweep over their heads. On the wall next to them is a giant stone fireplace, and at the far end of the room, a pair of glass doors opens onto a courtyard garden. At the center of it all, a magnolia tree, exactly like the one in the painting, stretches its branches toward the ceiling. Plump velvet cushions, perfect for reading, are piled around its roots.

"Where do we start?" Leonor asks. She pulls a book off one of the towers and flips through its crinkled pages.

Lizeth steps up to the tree and begins to climb, stopping to check inside a knot above the second branch.

Inés sneezes. "Does it have to be so dusty in here?" She runs a finger over a small statue of a dragon that rests on one of the desks. A flurry of sparks streams from the dragon's nostrils, and Inés pulls her hand away. "Eeep!"

One of the sparks flutters into the fireplace. Instantly, the fireplace crackles to life. Dazzling flames dance in the colors of the four Casitas.

Leonor drops the book she is holding and Lizeth jumps down from the magnolia tree.

"You don't think the clue is in *there*, do you?" Leonor asks, pointing to the fireplace.

"Dalia, go look," Inés says.

Dalia is already looking, but not in the fireplace. The flames have cast a glow over a sturdy and simple book stand. Closed on top is an old leather-bound book with stones—opals, sapphires, emeralds, and rubies—set into its cover. *The Bright and Brilliant History of the Fine and Ancient Institute for the Royal.*

The F.A.I.R. is where this journey started. Dalia hopes it's not where hers ends.

She opens the book.

The tinkling sound of distant bells fills the dark room as a flurry of fireflies flutters out from between the book's pages.

Words begin to appear in flickering yellow lights. *True treasure may be found where you picture yourself in time.*

Then the lights on the page go dim.

CHAPTER
12

Leonor rolls toward Dalia and pats her shoulder. "That was the clue, wasn't it?"

"You did it!" Lizeth says. "We're going to win!"

"She *helped*," Inés says. "I suppose." She shoves Dalia aside to examine the history book. She frowns when she sees the empty page.

"There's nothing there!" she says. "You ruined it! What did it say?"

Dalia could tell them anything now. But she

doesn't have to. It's as if the clue were perfectly designed to lead them astray. She only has to nudge them in the *wrong* direction. For once, her plan is working.

Yet, looking at the princesas' faces and the sparkle of their eyes in the firelight, she hesitates.

But why? Villains don't shrink from betrayal. Betrayal is one of the things villains do best.

"So?" Leonor asks. "Where do we go next?"

Dalia takes a deep breath. She blows the hair out of her face and recites the clue. *"True treasure may be found where you picture yourself in* time."

She draws out the last word, says it louder than the others in hopes it will lead the princesas straight to the clock tower. With any luck, the rest of the school will follow them there. Straight into Dalia's trap.

She reaches into her pocket and wraps her

fingers around the charcoal. There's just enough left to scribble out a note to the B.A.D. when the scheme succeeds.

"See yourself in time," Lizeth repeats, dropping cross-legged to the floor.

"Time," Inés says. She begins to pace. "It sounds like the clock tower . . ."

This has almost been too easy. Dalia picks up her lantern and hurries toward the door. "The clock tower. Of course!" she says. "Let's go. The other princesas will be right behind us."

"Wait." Inés stops her.

"We can't," Dalia insists. Once the princesas are inside the tower—once they're trapped—she'll break away and find Dominga.

"I wasn't finished," Inés says. "As I was saying, it *sounds* like the clock tower, but I think that's a trick."

Dalia forces a smile.

"Really, Inés, do you *still* think I'm trying to trick you? After we've come so far? Of course it's the clock tower. You heard the clue." She turns to Lizeth and Leonor. "You believe me, don't you?"

Lizeth and Leonor look at each other but won't meet Dalia's eyes. Lizeth fidgets with the lace on her sleeve. "You're very good at finding your way around the palace, but . . ."

Her voice falls away before she finishes the sentence. Leonor rolls forward and picks up where Lizeth left off. "But Inés is right. It seems like a trick."

"*You* think I'm playing a trick on you too?" Dalia can't decide whether she feels proud that the princesas see her for the villain she is or disappointed that she's not as sneaky as she thought.

Or maybe she's insulted that they still don't trust her. As far as they know, she's been nothing but helpful all evening.

"Not *you*," Leonor continues. "Profesora Colibrí. And not a trick exactly. More like a *test*. The clock tower is too obvious an answer. She'd want us to work harder to solve the last clue, don't you think? None of the other clues were that easy."

Dalia blinks back at them. She did not expect the princesas to be so cunning. Inside Dominga's spell book, Paloma wrote her top three Rules for Royalty. Dominga should scratch that list out and start another one. Rules for Villains. And at the top of the list, Dalia would write, *Never underestimate a princesa*.

"Well, where do *you* think we should go?" Dalia asks.

Footsteps thump down the hallway. They all look up. Even the toad.

"They've caught up," Inés says.

Lizeth jumps off the ground. The cushion she's been sitting on falls against Dalia's boot. "No! Not when we're so close!"

Leonor turns to Dalia. "We can still win, can't we? I want those gems."

Dalia closes her eyes, straining to listen to the sounds outside. "It won't take them long to get here," she says. "Even if they don't know about the passage through the painting."

"Then we better get moving," Inés says.

Leonor throws her arms up. "But *where*?"

Dalia doesn't care much about winning. But she realizes with growing panic that if the other princesas find them, and *everyone* refuses to follow her to the clock tower, it will be even harder, maybe impossible, to save this scheme.

Inés tugs the end of one of her coppery curls. "I think it's the portrait gallery," she says in a voice so unsure that Dalia almost can't believe it came out of Inés's mouth.

The portrait gallery is a long room with polished stone floors right off the castle's grand entrance. On its wood-paneled walls, gold frames hold portraits of each class of princesas, taken at their graduation, the moment they become really royal.

For once, Inés is right.

It's happened at the best possible time for the team, which makes it the *worst* possible time for Dalia.

"Picture yourself," Leonor says, nodding. "That's what the clue said, isn't it? Maybe it means a picture *of* ourselves."

Lizeth wraps her arms around Inés's shoulders and squeezes. *"In time,"* she adds. "Our portrait isn't hanging yet, but it will be someday. Inés, I think you're right!"

Inés shakes Lizeth's arms away. "Of course I'm right," she says, volume returning with her confidence. "You shouldn't sound so surprised."

Dalia kicks at the cushion that Lizeth was sitting on. Somehow, she's led the princesas straight to victory. No wonder the B.A.D. won't let her in.

She sinks to the ground. The corner of Dominga's spell book pokes her leg. "Ouch!"

She reaches into her pocket to adjust the book,

and as soon as her fingers touch the cover, she realizes, *Maybe there's still a way.*

She takes out the book and opens it to Paloma's map. "The portrait gallery," she agrees. "I know a shortcut."

CHAPTER 13

"We don't need another one of your shortcuts," Inés snaps at Dalia. "This time *I* know the way."

Inés's way will have them inside the portrait gallery after a journey down a winding hallway, three quick turns, and a short dash through the ballet studio. They'll arrive long before sunrise. Exactly what Dalia cannot let happen.

"But this isn't *my* shortcut," Dalia argues. She waves her hand over the map. "Dominga's sister drew it, and as you may have heard, she was the Fairest of the F.A.I.R., so I think she probably knew her way around the palace."

Of course Inés has heard. "Princesa Paloma? Let me see that."

Dalia pulls the book out of Inés's reach. "According to this map," she continues, tapping on the page, "we can go outside, cut through the sunken garden, and get straight to the portrait gallery through a hidden passage behind the shrubs. It'll be much faster."

Inés squints at the page, trying to read the map. But Dalia tilts it so she can't see. This is Dalia's last chance to earn her way into the B.A.D. She'll lead the princesas to the garden, pick the lock, then trap them inside. No one will come to rescue them until Señor De La Rosa returns at dawn to prune. By that time, Dalia and Dominga will be long gone, on their way to the B.A.D. with a dreadful story to tell. She won't have trapped all the princesas. Or even most of them. But three is better than none. Three must count for something.

"If we go my way—*Paloma's* way—we'll probably be the fastest team to ever win the Starlight Search," Dalia continues. "I wonder if Profesora Colibrí keeps a record book. Can't you just imagine your name in it? The fastest team ever?"

Inés turns to Dalia. "What are you waiting for?"

Before Inés can change her mind, Dalia springs to her feet and leads the Opal princesas out the glass doors and onto the courtyard. She hangs back to scribble another tiny bat on the door frame but only has time to draw a single wing before Inés screeches, "Hurry!"

They make their way across the courtyard,

down a ramp, and along a path that loops around the palace. Dalia leads them past the tennis courts; past the observatory, where Profesora Astra studies the sky; and past the dense ancient forest at the edge of the palace grounds.

Finally, the iron gates of the sunken garden come into view. Inés sprints out ahead of the group.

"I'm going to be the first inside!" she calls without looking back.

But when she tries to open the gate, she finds it locked. She shakes it, then turns back to Dalia, glowering. "We can't get through," she says through clenched teeth. "I told you we should have gone my way. Now what are we going to do?"

Dalia shakes her curls out of her face. She straightens her cloak across her shoulders. She smiles.

"Why are you smiling?" Lizeth asks. "We're stuck. We'll have to turn back."

"I hate to say it," Leonor adds, "but maybe we should have followed Inés."

Dalia does not respond to them. Instead, she looks at Inés. "Do you have a hairpin I could borrow?"

Leonor and Lizeth swivel their heads around. "Huh?" they ask in unison.

Dalia's request seems to surprise Inés too, and it takes her several moments to reply. When she does, it's to sneer at Dalia's tangles. "I don't blame you for wanting to do *something* about that hair," she says. "But now is not the time, and to be honest, it's going to take more than a hairpin."

Lizeth coughs.

"Not for my hair," Dalia says. "For the lock. I'll use the pin to open it."

Without taking her eyes off Dalia, Inés pulls a gold hairpin from her tiara.

Dalia takes it and bends it straight.

"What are you doing?" Inés gasps. "I didn't say you could break it!"

Dalia sticks the pin into the lock.

"Wait." Leonor places her hand over Dalia's. "Are you sure about this? It seems a little, I don't know . . ."

"Wicked?" Lizeth suggests. "Rotten? Sneaky? Unprincesslike?"

"Don't be ridiculous," Inés says, finally understanding what Dalia means to do. "A true princesa is resourceful. What would Profesora Colibrí think if we *gave up*?" She nudges Dalia. "Keep going!"

Leonor drops her hand. Dalia twists and wiggles the hairpin until the lock clicks and then pops open.

"I guess that means we're in," Leonor says as the gate swings free.

"Thanks to *me*," Inés says, swiping the ruined hairpin out of Dalia's hand. "We wouldn't have gotten through if *I* hadn't been prepared." She pushes past Leonor.

They head into the garden. Dalia counts their steps, trying to decide when to make her next move.

"I've come here lots of times to paint," Leonor says. "And I've never seen a door. I can't believe I've missed it."

Dalia swallows. Leonor hasn't seen the door because the door doesn't exist. "It's over there, behind the fountain," she lies. "Near that shrub that looks like a witch."

A cricket chirps. The toad croaks back at it.

"Not now, Dominga," Inés says.

Dalia glances over her shoulder at the gate. This should be far enough.

"Oh, drat!" she exclaims, hoping her voice sounds genuinely upset. She stomps her foot to make the performance more convincing.

The three Opal princesas turn to look at her.

"What now?" Inés asks.

"I forgot to close the gate. Now the other teams can follow us and take advantage of our quick thinking."

Inés scowls. "Am I the only person who can do anything right around here?" She waves her hands, shooing Dalia away. "Go! Lock it!"

Dalia is already hurrying back the way she came. "I won't be long!"

Now she'll slip through the gate and refasten the lock. The princesas will be trapped inside.

But after a few more steps, she skitters to a stop. She hears something. She must be imagining it.

But she isn't.

Humming.

And then Eloísa's horribly cheerful chirp.

"Dalia? Is that you? We've been looking everywhere!"

CHAPTER 14

If Dalia keeps on walking toward the gates, she'll run straight into Eloísa. If she turns around, she'll have to face Inés. So she stops and stares up at the hedge that's trimmed to look like the princesa whose brothers were turned into swans. She wouldn't mind if a witch turned her into a swan right about now. She'd soar over the garden walls and straight to the B.A.D., picking Dominga up along the way.

Although with their luck, the villains of the B.A.D. probably wouldn't want swans on their grounds any more than they seem to want her.

And anyway, no witch is coming to her rescue.

"Wait!" Eloísa calls out when she spots her. "Dalia, it's us!"

Dalia takes a deep breath and turns. Following close behind Eloísa are Carmen and Marisol, each carrying a lantern.

Carmen looks Dalia over, from the toes of her scuffed boots to the tip of her tarnished tiara.

"See?" Carmen says. "I told you she wasn't in trouble. She just wanted to be on her own. So weird. We've wasted enough time. Let's get going to the portrait gallery."

Dalia is used to being called weird. That's what people always say about villains. So Carmen's words don't bother her.

Much.

In fact, the sooner Carmen and the Emerald princesas leave, the better. If they make any more noise, Inés will hear and come running back.

But then again, Dalia wonders, *why shouldn't the Emeralds and Opals meet up in the garden?* It would be a perfectly unpleasant twist. If she can trap *both* teams, she'll have an even bigger plot to report.

"Wait," she says. "If you're looking for the portrait gallery, I know a shortcut. That way." She points in the direction she's just come from.

"But why didn't you wait for us?" Eloísa persists. "I thought we were going to search together, as a team. We've been looking all over for you. And when I found the trail of bats you left behind, I was certain you wanted us to find you."

The bats. Dalia's stomach sinks.

"I KNEW it!"

Dalia covers her face with her hands. "Oh no."

Inés strides toward them, face bright and pink. She holds her lantern out in front of her, and it throws a sharp streak of light across her cheek. Tiny pebbles fly out from underneath her slippers.

"Inés?" Eloísa says, shrinking backward.

"I knew it," Inés repeats, glaring at Dalia. "You were helping them all along. Spying on us! Leaving them a trail so they could follow me to the treasure!"

Dalia laughs. She can't help it. It comes out like a jackal's bark. "Follow you? If I were following you, we'd still be in the carriage house right now. You couldn't have gotten this far without me." Villains never get the credit they deserve.

"I thought the clue was in the carriage house too," Carmen admits.

Eloísa's hand flies over her mouth. "Wait, you

135

led her here? But why?" She looks up at Dalia. Her face crumples. "How could you do this? I stuck up for you!" The bow tie at her neck droops like a wilted flower.

Dalia turns from Eloísa to Inés. Every answer seems wrong, and every moment is pushing her further away from the B.A.D.

"Did you lock the gate yet?" Leonor rolls under the sweetly perfumed branch of a lilac tree, Lizeth beside her.

She stops short when she notices the others. Lizeth holds her lantern up toward the Emerald princesas. "What's going on?"

Inés narrows her eyes. "I'll tell you what's going on," she says. "Dalia here has been helping the Emerald princesas all along. Just wait until Profesora Colibrí hears about this. Those kinds of tricks don't belong at the F.A.I.R., and neither do you!"

Leonor moves between Inés and Dalia. "Really, Inés, don't you think you're being a little dramatic? Dalia isn't even a part of our Casita, and she has been helping us this entire night. If it weren't for her, we never would have made it this far."

Eloísa sobs.

Marisol shakes her head. "I knew I should have stayed in bed."

Inés spins in front of Leonor, her gown twirling out around her ankles. "I knew all along she was up to something. You don't believe me? Well, there's one way to prove it."

Before Dalia realizes what's happening, and before she has a chance to squirm out of the way, Inés snatches Dominga's spell book.

"No!" Dalia screams. Her stomach somersaults as Inés flips through its pages. A true villain would never lose hold of her secrets so easily.

But Inés doesn't seem interested in secrets at all. She's just whipping through the pages as she continues to rant. "She *says* she's leading us to a shortcut, but we've looked all over, and there isn't another way out of this garden."

Leonor lowers her eyes. "It's true, Dalia," she says. "If there's a hidden door somewhere around here, we can't find it."

Inés keeps flipping. "Aha!" She turns the book around. It's open to the pages with the map of the palace drawn inside. "Just as I suspected. Here's the sunken garden"—she jabs the page angrily with her finger—"and there is no shortcut *anywhere!*"

Dalia grabs for the book, and now that she's made her point, Inés doesn't resist.

"Don't even try to deny it," Inés says, one hand on her hip. "It's all right there."

"Dalia?" Leonor asks.

Eloísa pulls at her tie, loosening it. "Will someone *please* explain what's going on?"

"Yes, Dalia," Inés says, shining her lantern onto Dalia's face. "Why don't you explain?" Then she stops. She squints. "Wait a minute. That picture in your locket. I finally remember where I've seen it before." Her voice grows louder and her eyes glint. But before she can finish speaking . . .

BOOM! A crash like thunder comes from behind the hedges. Gold and silver sparks explode all around them.

CHAPTER 15

The princesas scream. Bright lights—pink and orange and turquoise—flash over the garden. Dalia shields her eyes with Dominga's spell book.

Inés whirls into her. "Get me out of here!" she cries.

The princesas take off in all directions, calling out to one another. Leonor's lantern flickers briefly, but its light is swallowed by the thick purple smoke that begins to swirl through the garden. It smells a little like burnt sugar, not unlike what Dalia smelled earlier when she found Dominga in the bakery.

She feels a sharp, sudden tug at the bottom of her cloak. She tumbles to the ground and rolls under the outstretched wing of one of the swan-shaped hedges. The wing seems to bend and encircle her, shielding her from the smoke and sparkle outside.

"Who's there?"

She lifts her lantern.

Dominga blinks back at her through round, gold-rimmed glasses, smudged with ash. She pulls them off and wipes the lenses with the edge of her skirt, which, Dalia notices, is speckled with tiny burn holes.

"I should have known," Dalia says. She peeks through the leaves. "Your secret recipe?"

Small explosions light up the trees, sending showers of golden glittery sparks down over the garden. In a flash of orange light, Dalia sees Inés run into a flowerpot. It tips over, spilling soil over her shoes.

"These were my favorite pair!" she yells.

Dalia begins to cackle. But she puts her hand over her mouth and lets her laugh turn into a polite sort of cough when she realizes Dominga isn't even smiling.

"You probably want this back," Dalia says, holding the spell book out to her.

Dominga takes the book and looks down at it, running her hand over the cover. Then she looks back at Dalia.

"Why didn't you tell me?" she asks. "About your mom, I mean."

Dalia draws her knees up to her chest and rests her chin on top of them. She has been expecting this question. But that doesn't make it any easier to answer.

"I haven't told anyone," Dalia mumbles. "Not since I went to live with my abuelos. They made me promise not to. They said it was for the best . . ."

Her voice dwindles. She has told the truth, but it isn't *all* of the truth. Dominga nods but doesn't say anything. She seems to be waiting for more.

Villains are very clever that way. They can see through half-truths and distractions probably better than anyone.

Dalia sighs. "What would you have thought if I'd told you? You've had to learn to be a villain all by yourself, but I don't have any excuse. My mother is the director of the B.A.D.! And even *she* thinks I'm not good enough—or, I mean, *bad* enough."

Dominga finds a roly-poly in the dirt, picks it up, and drops it into her hand. It curls into a tiny ball. Still remembering the toad in Inés's pocket, Dalia half expects the real Dominga to eat the bug. Instead, once it unrolls, she lets it crawl up and down her long fingers.

"My mom doesn't seem to think I'm good enough either," Dominga says finally. "Especially compared to Princesa Perfecta." *Princesa Perfecta* is what Dominga calls her older sister.

Dalia straightens. "So, you're not mad?"

"I felt pretty bad when I first saw the locket," Dominga admits. "I was worried that you didn't trust me. That maybe you still didn't believe I'm a true villain." Her glasses slip, and she pushes them back up her nose. "And then I decided to prove it to you."

Dalia peers at her through the dark curtain of her hair. "It sounds like you felt the same way I did."

Dominga nods. "But also kind of different."

Another explosion roars across the garden. More sparks rain down. Inés yowls again.

Dalia cackles, and this time, Dominga joins in.

"I'd say you've definitely proven it," Dalia congratulates her. "To me and, soon, to the B.A.D. How much of that stuff did you make?"

Dominga drops the roly-poly back onto the dirt, then pulls a small bundle, rolled up in an old flour sack, from inside the folds of her cloak. She grins. "Enough to get us out of here and to lock the princesas inside before the smoke clears."

"Dreadfully crafty," Dalia says.

"Shall we?" Dominga suggests.

They crawl out from under the swan's wing and stand. Dominga unrolls the flour sack. Dalia shakes the dried leaves off her skirt. Her lantern shines dully in the smoky air.

Dominga takes a pinch of sparkling powder from her bundle and prepares to toss it. "You'd better hold your breath," she advises.

But before she can throw, another sound cuts through the commotion. "Princesas, what is the meaning of this?"

CHAPTER 16

Dalia grips Dominga's hand. Dominga squeezes back. They both let go and turn in the direction of Profesora Colibrí's voice.

They can't see her at first, with the lights still flashing and the smoke still swirling. But slowly, a violet glow begins to grow around her fan. Profesora Colibrí raises her arm.

The smoke and lights and sparkles start to spiral above her, as if being pulled toward the fan, twisting together like taffy. Then, with the flick of her wrist, Profesora Colibrí sends the long magical twine into the clouds.

She nods in satisfaction before fluttering her fan toward the shrubs. Their branches come alive with tiny twinkling lights. A breeze hits them, and the lights flicker with a sound like bells tinkling.

It's then that Dalia realizes Profesora Colibrí has not come alone. Behind her are the rest of the first-year princesas, some in their pajamas, others in their gowns. They carry lanterns and hold tight to maps. Their tiaras glisten.

Leonor, holding a garden rake in front of her like a sword, gazes up at Profesora Colibrí, trying to catch her breath. Carmen, beside her, clutches an acorn in her fist, ready to throw.

Inés wriggles out from underneath a garden bench. The front of her gown is streaked with mud, and she is missing a glove. She catches sight of Dominga and wrinkles her nose in confusion. Then her eyes begin to widen.

"If you're *there*, then . . ."

With her gloved hand, she reaches into her pocket and pulls out the toad, still wearing her tiny wire glasses. Inés howls. "Get it away from me!"

She drops the toad, then slaps her hand against her skirt as if trying to wipe away the feel of the animal's bumpy skin.

"It's time I get home anyway," the toad croaks. "My family will be worried. Thank you for a most magnificent evening." The bit of black lace she has been wearing catches on a twig and slips off as the toad hops through a bush.

Dalia and Dominga wave goodbye.

Inés marches toward them. "Everything has gone completely wrong, and it's all because of you!"

Profesora Colibrí pats the back of her indigo bun to smooth down the strands that shook loose while she was clearing Dominga's magic. "Princesa Inés, are you well?" She flutters her fan in front of her face.

Inés sniffs and stretches out her neck. "No, I am not well, Profesora," she says. "And it's because of *them*." She points to Dalia and Dominga. "They've been up to something dreadful. *As usual.*"

Profesora Colibrí looks back at them. "Is this true?"

Inés doesn't let them answer. "Of course it's true. First, I caught Dalia sneaking around our suite *before* the midnight chimes had rung."

"And what did you do then?" Dominga asks. "*Before* the chimes had rung."

Profesora Colibrí waits for Inés to continue. Inés blinks fast, realizing, perhaps, that if she's not careful, she'll wind up admitting that she too was up before she was supposed to be. She closes her mouth.

Truly magical, Dalia thinks.

"You were saying?" Dominga says.

"About what happened *before* the chimes?" Dalia adds.

Inés frowns. "The time isn't important. Because what happened next was that we followed Dalia to the first clue and then she—I mean *I*—I mean . . ."

She pauses, unwilling to admit it was Dalia who figured out what the clue in the music salon meant.

"What was that?" Leonor asks, moving forward. "I didn't quite hear what you were saying."

Inés's cheeks flush bright pink. She looks up again at Profesora Colibrí. "It doesn't matter! Because after that, Dalia brought us here and told us there was a shortcut when there obviously isn't, so we all got stuck, and then *she* showed up." She stops and points at Dominga. "And the next thing we knew, there was this terrifying explosion. My ears are still ringing, and I'll never get this smell out of my dress. What even *is* it?"

Profesora Colibrí snaps her fan shut. She raps it against her palm. She turns to Dominga.

"If that's true, Princesa . . ."

Dalia feels Dominga stiffen beside her and suck in a tense breath. Dominga's mother has warned her that if she gets caught trying any villain tricks, she'll be sent back home to manage Princesa Paloma's letters. Forever.

Dalia tries to imagine school without Dominga and can't. If Dominga gets kicked out, she'll go with her. They'll keep on trying to get to the B.A.D. Together.

"Yes, Profesora?" Dominga says, her voice brittle.

"Tell her!" Inés snaps. Her nostrils flare.

Profesora Colibrí flicks her fan open again and flutters it. "If that's true, Princesa," she continues, "then you deserve our applause!" She turns toward the rest of the princesas, who have been watching in curious and confused silence. Once she has their attention, she stands between Dalia and Dominga and slips her fan into the waistband of her skirt. She takes Dominga's hand and raises it. "For summoning help when you needed it most. It is a true skill to know when you can't solve a problem on your own!"

Next, she raises Dalia's arm. "And for bringing us all together and reminding us that a true princesa is never alone. And none of us win unless we win together. Ten gems to each of the Casitas!"

Inés's mouth hangs open. *"What?"* She recovers quickly, then her mouth curls into a dangerous smile. She takes Dalia's free hand and raises it. "And *I'm* the one who invited Dalia to join us!"

No one really hears her, though. They've already erupted into cheers.

Dominga cringes. Dalia squeezes her eyes shut. "Not again," she mutters.

Profesora Colibrí hoots. It is impeccable owl-speak for "Kindly inform Chef Luís-Esteban that the feast he has prepared for the portrait gallery should instead be delivered to the sunken garden. We'll enjoy it under the light of the Cloudberry Moon."

An owl swoops low over their heads on its way toward the palace.

CHAPTER 17

Dalia and Dominga find the hedge that's trimmed to look like the princesa who soared on the back of an eagle. They sit on either side of her.

In the sunken garden, princesas stand in despicably orderly lines to choose pastries from Chef Luís-Esteban's kitchen. Then, one at a time, they dip a ladle into a crystal bowl and fill their glasses with fizzy pink fruit punch.

With a flick of her fan, Profesora Colibrí

summons a breeze that blows in a swirl of fireflies like the ones that flew from the pages of the F.A.I.R.'s history book: icy blue, mint green, glowing white, and soft pink. They flit in and out of the branches and land on the princesas' tiaras.

Señor De La Rosa has invited the bunnies to join the celebration. They hop among the princesas' feet and nibble on the cabbages and carrots he has arranged on a picnic blanket to distract them from his perfectly manicured flowers. Crickets chirp and a mockingbird sings. Every now and then, the remnants of Dominga's secret recipe explode into fireworks, sending glimmering sparks into the air.

Farther than they've ever seemed before, the towers of the B.A.D. rise stark against the Cloudberry Moon.

"What a disaster," Dalia admits after surveying the scene.

"I never thought things could be quite this awful," Dominga admits. "Or is it this *wonderful*? Anyway, you know what I mean."

Dalia nods. Unfortunately, she does.

A pink firefly floats by. Eloísa, with Doña Kettlecorn the bunny tucked into the Emerald sash around her waist, leaps and catches it inside her cupped hands.

"Oh, Dalia! There you are," she says. "I never doubted you for a moment. I just *knew* you had to be up to something amazing. I've always wanted a surprise party. This is just like one, only about a thousand times *better*! Remind me when we get back to the suite, there's a project I want to talk to you about."

The firefly escapes through a space between Eloísa's fingers. "Oh!" She scampers after it.

Dalia groans.

Not far from where they sit, Inés straightens her tiara. She bends to pluck a starflower, smells it, then tucks it behind her ear. "And that's how I knew it *couldn't* be in the carriage house," she tells Princesa Jacinta. "It had to be in the library. And, of course, I found a secret passage."

Inés glances up and notices Dalia and Dominga watching. She flutters her eyelashes and raises her voice. "The palace is full of secrets, wouldn't you agree, Princesa Dalia?"

Dalia looks away. "I knew you would recognize my mother," she whispers to Dominga. "Any true villain would."

Dominga smiles.

"But I still can't figure out . . ."

"How *Inés* knew?" Dominga finishes her sentence. "I've been wondering the same thing."

"Do you think she'll tell everyone?" Dalia asks.

"Not if she doesn't want to admit that she recognized the director of the B.A.D."

From the other end of the garden, Eloísa calls out, "Dalia! Dominga! Come down to the fountain. We're starting a sing-along."

Leonor has begun to set up an easel. "And I'm going to draw caricatures!"

Dalia shudders. "I cannot bear a sing-along," she says. "Or caricatures."

"Absolutely not," Dominga agrees. She tears a blank page out of her spell book. "We have more important business."

Dalia turns. "We do?"

"A full report on tonight's events, of course," she says. "To send to the B.A.D."

Dalia looks away. "Very funny," she says glumly.

"I'm not being funny," Dominga insists.

"But you said it yourself," Dalia argues. "This whole evening has been disastrously delightful."

There is another small explosion. Princesas squeal as sparks fly out behind them.

"Not *entirely* delightful," Dominga says. "For one thing, Inés is right about the smell. It'll never come out. And it looks like the bunnies have discovered Señor De La Rosa's petunias."

Dalia twists a strand of hair around her finger. "And if you think about it, we did manage to trap all the princesas in here."

"We did!" Dominga shouts, leaping off the eagle.

Dalia drops noiselessly down beside her. "Let's start writing, shall we?"

When they are finished, Dominga rolls the paper up tightly. Dalia pulls a loose thread from her gown, then taps on her boot. Don Ignacio pokes his head out the top.

"Another delivery for you," Dalia says. She uses the thread to fasten the letter to his back. "You know where to go."

Don Ignacio scurries away as even more fireworks light up the sky.

To Dalia and Dominga,

We have come to look forward to these visits from your clever lizard friend. We read with interest your most recent dispatch from the F.A.I.R. While you have managed to pull off a quite clever caper, we regret to say that it was only fairly dreadful. Your application for admission is denied.

Awfully yours,
The B.A.D.

PS We must admit, we find your persistence *terribly* admirable. True villains never give up.

Read on for a sneak peek at Dalia and Dominga's next wicked plot:

BAD PRINCESSES 3:
PARTY CRASHERS

Princesa Jacinta, torchlight glowing in her eyes, comes to the end of her story. "And the witch, disguised as an owl, always reveals herself with a long, lonely whistle."

Just then, a high-pitched shriek slices through the darkness.

Everyone screams.

Everyone except Dalia and Dominga.

They have already guessed that the witch in their midst is actually Princesa Candelaria, crouching at the edge of the campfire circle.

"I wouldn't mind if an owl visited me at night," Dalia whispers to Dominga. They sit just outside the circle, a little apart from the rest of the first-year princesas. "Even if it *was* a witch. Owls have special wings that let them fly silently to swoop down on their prey."

A lizard pokes his head out of the top of Dalia's black boot. He sticks his tongue out.

"Don't worry, Don Ignacio," Dalia says, running a finger over his head. "I'd never let an owl come for *you*."

Dominga pulls her black velvet cloak tighter around her shoulders. She was hopeful when Profesora Colibrí, the head teacher, announced that their evening at the base of Mount Linda Vista would end with scary stories around the campfire. It might even make up for the swimming in crystal waters (too refreshing), the roasting of marshmallows (too gooey), and the singing of camp songs (too chirpy) they'd already been forced to endure that day.

"We might as well listen for a while," she had told Dalia. Scary would be a welcome relief from the Fine and Ancient Institute for the Royal's usual sticky-sweetness.

The campfire crackles. Orange-red flames dance inside a ring of stones. Violet sparks leap out and flit toward the stars. Dominga follows them with her eyes, up, up to where the ghostly towers of the Bewitched Academy for the Dreadful rise against the full moon.

That is where Dalia and Dominga truly belong. They are not royals-in-training like the rest of these princesas. They are villains—secret villains—but villains nonetheless. Yet their hopes of getting into the B.A.D. seem as slim as one of these stories being actually creepy. The B.A.D. is notoriously selective. Only the most truly awful and desperately dangerous students are offered admission.

And so far, Dalia and Dominga have not proven themselves good enough—that is, *bad* enough— to attend. But they have not given up. Villains never do.

"Thank you, Casita Sapphire, for that won- derfully chilling tale," Profesora Colibrí says, applauding. Jacinta and Candelaria curtsy as the rest of the princesas clap. "Ten gems for your chalice." The clapping from Casita Sapphire grows louder. On the first day of school, Profesora Colibrí assigned each new princesa to a cottage: Ruby, Sapphire, Emerald, or Opal. For every noble deed accomplished, a princesa can earn gems for her Casita's chalice. The house with the most gems at the end of the term will earn the privilege of venturing into the village beyond the palace's walls.

"Would Casita Opal like to terrify us next?" Profesora Colibrí asks.

"Not likely," Dominga mutters. Dalia snickers.

"What was that, Princesa?" The profesora leans her ear toward Dominga. "Will you be telling a story on behalf of your Casita?"

Before Dominga can reply, a tall princesa with coppery curls springs to her feet. "Of course not," she says, grabbing the torch from Jacinta. "I've been preparing our story for weeks." Princesa Inés is determined to be named the Fairest of the F.A.I.R., the most perfect of all the princesas, by the time they graduate.

"Of course," Profesora Colibrí says, and settles back into her camp chair.

Dalia gathers up the folds of her satin gown, a green so dark it is almost black. "I think we've stayed long enough, don't you agree?" she whispers.

Dominga pushes her glasses up higher on her nose. "*Too* long," she whispers back. They have a plot to set afoot.

As Inés clears her throat and begins her story, Dalia and Dominga sneak away into the shadows.

Four round tents stand in a line at the edge of the campsite. Silky streamers fly from the tops of each one: red, blue, green, and white. Inside the tents, lanterns twinkle over cushioned cots. A satin sleep mask sits atop every plumped pillow.

Dalia and Dominga scurry past to the smaller, plainer tent, where earlier, they all stored their luggage. Hiking gowns hang from racks, ready to be worn the next day. A day that will no doubt be warm and gold-tinged just like every other day at the F.A.I.R.

Or it would be, Dominga thinks, *if she and Dalia weren't about to roll in like storm clouds.*

The idea came to her when they arrived that afternoon. As the others began unpacking, Dominga swiped a pair of scissors from Valentina, the Ruby princesa who is always busy with some new craft. She wouldn't miss it. She'd packed two more pairs. "One for paper, one for fabric, and one for embroidery," Valentina had explained.

It reminded Dominga of the spoons in Chef Luís-Esteban's kitchen. The wooden spoon for stirring caramel. The slotted spoon for lifting potatoes out of boiling water. The long-handled ladle for scooping up soup. Not to mention the endless spoons for eating. The kitchen will be one of the few places Dominga misses when she and Dalia finally receive their invitations to the B.A.D.

Which they surely will after this scheme. Never mind that all their others have turned out horribly, disastrously, gruesomely *nice*.

Standing in front of the rack of gowns, Dalia taps on the toe of her boot. Don Ignacio peeks out and tests the air with his tongue.

"Where shall we begin?" Dalia asks the lizard. "You can pick first."